For Catherine and Ellen - love, Christine.

For my fabulous parents - all my love, Sarah.

Text copyright © 1998 by Christine Morton
Illustration copyright © 1998 by Sarah Barringer
First published in Great Britain in 1998 by Macmillan Children's Books, a division of
Macmillan Publishers Limited.
First Published in the United States by Holiday House, Inc., in 1998.
All Rights Reserved
Printed in Belgium
Library of Congress Cataloging-in-Publication Data
Morton, Christine.
    Picnic farm / Christine Morton & Sarah Barringer.
      p.   cm.
    Summary: Children visiting a farm enjoy a picnic made up of all
the foods the farm produces.
    ISBN 0-8234-1332-2
    [1. Picnicking—Fiction. 2. Farm life—Fiction.] I. Barringer,
Sarah, ill. II. Title.
PZ7.M845835Pi 1998
[E]—dc21

97-10880
CIP
AC

Picnic Farm

Christine Morton and Sarah Barringer

Holiday House/New York

Here are the children at the farm.

Here is the farmer showing them round,

and these are the things they saw...

A sheep, a sheep—a shy old sheep.

A hen, a hen-a squabbling hen.

Trees, trees—tall fruit trees.

Bees, bees—buzzing bees.

A cow, a cow-a chewing cow.

A churn, a churn–a turning churn.

Wheat, wheat—waving wheat.

Grass, grass–good green grass.

Here are the children out in the yard.

Here is the farmer leading the way,

and these are the things they brought . . .

A rug, a rug—of wool from the sheep.

Eggs, eggs-laid by the hen.

Plums, plums - picked from the trees.

honey

Honey, honey—made by the bees.

Milk, milk-milked from the cow.

Butter, butter—made in the churn.

Bread, bread-made from the wheat.

And a chocolate cake
that the children made!

Here is the stream they sat beside.

They ate and they ate and
they ate and they ate . . .

...and they all fell asleep

on the good green grass.